Making Nice

by Alan Haehnel

Baker's Plays
7611 Sunset Blvd.
Los Angeles, CA 90042
bakersplays.com

Making Nice was originally produced at Hartford High School, Hartford, VT on February 19th, 1998. It was directed by the author. The cast was as follows:

BARBARA . . . . Shanna Clark
ELLEN . . . . Ariana Keyser
JASON . . . . Josh Abetti
STEWART . . . . Chris MacDonald
MARLY . . . . Morgan Haynes
HETTY . . . . Emily Wood
CLAIRE . . . . Sarah Abetti
TIMPANI PLAYER . . . . Nabil Maynard
HORSE HEAD . . . . Tom Loudon
HORSE BUTT . . . . Allison Cameron
MARY . . . . Faith Wood
SARAH . . . . Beth Collette
WIND WOMEN . . . . Caitlin Beidler, Christina Clark,
                 Sarah Wilson, Liz Wyzik, Beth Collette
WOLVES/DEMONS . . Tyler Coutermanche, Faith Wood,
                    Dan Araujo, Carma Gilchrist
ANGELS . . . Sarah Montouri, Kristin Hyra, Jessica Poludin
OLD WOMEN . . . . Elizabeth Lerner, Irina Skowronski
"TECHIE" . . . . Jolene Rice

CHARACTERS

BARBARA CRAMER – the director
ELLEN – the stage manager, "Zeitgeist"
JASON – plays Marcus
MARLY – an OSHAT representative
STEWART – Marly's partner
HETTY – the costume designer/builder
CLAIRE – plays Cybeline
TIMPANI PLAYER
HORSE HEAD
HORSE BUTT
MARY – a wolf who is also Claire's understudy
SARAH – a wind woman
JANET – a "techie"
CHRIS – a wind woman
NORM – a wolf
ROBERT – a wolf
PETER – an old man
SALLY – an old woman
SHIRLEY – a wind woman
MARTHA – an old woman
DONALD – a wolf
MARIA – a woman in white
BRIDGET – a woman in white

(Casting Note: all characters but Jason and Claire could be, with changes in character names, played as either male or female.)

Making Nice contains a tragic "play within the play" which, because so little of it is actually seen, allows for variety and creativity in costuming and cast size. One can imagine, for instance, that this tragedy requires elaborate costumes and a cast of sixty (thus filling the stage with spectacle during crowd scenes); or one can imagine that the tragedy uses simple costumes and a cast just large enough to fill the designated speaking parts.

MAKING NICE

*(Curtain opens to darkness. We hear the long, lonely whistle
of a cold wind and the shake of bare branches. Slowly, cold light
reveals a forbidding set: snow-covered rocks stage left and right,
a rickety bridge center stage, trees in the background. A white-
robed timpani player, standing on a rocky platform, bangs
heavily on his drum, signalling the entrance of the wind women.
Their blue, flowing costumes swirl as they dance around the set
in a spinning pattern. In their hands they hold sticks with long
flowing swatches of fabric. From offstage and from the wind
women come more wintry sounds — crackling branches, dry
and blowing leaves, wind. The set, the drum, the sounds, the
wind women, the blue light, all combine to foreshadow tragedy.
At one point during this opening, one of the wind women trips
and falls. Shortly after, Claire enters, looking bewildered,
bedraggled, and lost. Her costume indicates royalty, but it is
torn as if she has been long hours struggling through brambles.)*

CLAIRE. Where am I? Oh, where am I? *(Another character,
dark and menacing and slinking — a wolf — moves quickly in the
background.)* What was that? Oh, I should never have left my
home. *(Another wolf enters. Clearly, they are stalking Claire, but not
yet attacking.)* Oh, no! No, stay away from me! *(The timpani
builds louder, along with the wailing. There is a long howl from one of the
wolves. Claire tries to run, but she is cut off from any escape by two more
wolves. The circle tightens, drawing closer.)* Stay away! Oh, please,
Marcus ... Please find me! *(The wolves tense, then attack. Claire
screams as she sinks beneath them.)*
BARBARA. *(From the back of the auditorium, walking up onto the
stage, screaming.)* No! No, no, no, no, no, no, no-no, no. No!
(To Claire.) No. There is a definite problem here. *(To the light
booth.)* Give me some light!

(The lights come up full; everyone but Barbara winces at the glare. By this point, all of the other cast members have come out from the wings dressed in full makeup and elaborate costumes indicating that they are involved in a heavy tragedy of some sort.)

BARBARA. *(To the wolves.)* Get ... get out of my way. Sit. *(They sit down in front of her.)* Not here! Go! *(Claire starts to leave.)* No, you stay. Stand right there. *(To the whole cast.)* I need it absolutely and completely quiet right now! *(Everyone freezes and goes silent for a beat. The timpani player accidentally drops his mallet on his drum. Barbara stomps up to where he is.)*
TIMPANI PLAYER. I'm sorry. I didn't mean to. It slipped. *(Barbara grabs the mallets from him.)*
BARBARA. With a little effort, these things could go in places you cannot begin to imagine. Understand?
TIMPANI PLAYER. Sorry.
BARBARA. Be silent. *(Turning to walk back to Claire.)* Claire. Claire. Oh, my dear Claire. Tell me this: what is the first line of this scene? What do you say when you enter? *(To the cast.)* Silence!
CLAIRE. When I enter?
BARBARA. Yes.
CLAIRE. I say, *(Becoming suddenly dramatic, as if playing the scene.)* "Where am I? Where am I? Oh, Where am I?"
BARBARA. Oh, I see. Then, can you tell me why, when I was standing in the back of this theater, why do you suppose that the first word I heard you utter at the beginning of this very crucial, very dramatic scene, was ... "pajama"?
CLAIRE. Pajama?
BARBARA. Yes, pajama!
CLAIRE. I guess I'm not enunciating very well. Sorry.
BARBARA. And then you said it again. You said, "Pajama. Pajama. Oh, pajama!" *(There is a snickering from the crowd behind them. Barbara whirls in the direction of the noise.)* You think that's funny? Huh? *(Going to one of the "wind players," the one who fell*

down — Sarah.) Do you think that's funny? Stand up. Come here. Do you think the fact that I heard her say "pajama" is funny?

SARAH. Well, sort of.

BARBARA. (*After a pause and then a smile.*) It could be. It really could. (*She starts to laugh, as does the rest of the cast with her.*) I mean, imagine starting this very eerie, dramatic scene with the word "pajama." That's really pretty funny. But do you know what makes it (*Suddenly angry, no longer laughing.*) *not* funny? Hm? Do you?

SARAH. No.

BARBARA. When we're not doing a comedy! When the audience is supposed to cower in fear, to feel afraid for the character, to perhaps feel on the verge of tears, and, instead, it laughs ... that is not funny. That is terrible. Agreed?

SARAH. Yes. Agreed.

BARBARA. And how soon do we have an audience? Hm?

SARAH. Tomorrow.

BARBARA. See, that is not funny. You know what else is not funny, Sarah?

SARAH. No.

BARBARA. The fact that you are supposed to come out resembling a fierce and howling wind. That's what the script calls for — a "fierce and howling wind." How would you characterize your performance, especially when you fell down? Would that be a "fierce and howling wind" sort of thing? Would it?

SARAH. I don't know.

BARBARA. You don't? You don't? Well, I do! That was not a fierce and howling wind. That was a sickly spring breeze. A bumbling, tripping push of air. A mild exhalation from an asthmatic old sloth! All of you! Do you want to know what else is not funny the day before we open? Huh? "Pajama" is not funny! A slight breeze is not funny. An entire cast sleepwalking, a timpani player with the rhythmic concentration of an epileptic woodchuck, a cast of wolves who act as menacing as a tribe of Beenie Babies ... all of that is not funny. The night before we open, that is pitiful. Disgusting. Vomit inducing. Ellen! Ellen, where are you?

ELLEN. (*Coming from offstage, appearing behind Barbara.*) I'm here.

BARBARA. Don't sneak up on me. Where were you?

ELLEN. I was ...

BARBARA. Never mind. I don't care. I need everybody out here. Get everybody together. I'm leaving.

ELLEN. You're ... leaving? Barbara ... ?

BARBARA. Ellen, I am going to the bathroom. Did everybody hear that? I am leaving to go to the bathroom now! Is that all right, Ellen? Am I allowed?

ELLEN. I'm sorry, Barbara. When you said you were leaving, I thought ...

BARBARA. You were hoping I meant forever, weren't you? Well, no such luck.

ELLEN. Barbara, that is not what I was ...

BARBARA. I'll be back in five minutes. Have everybody out here and quiet when I get back.

ELLEN. Crew?

BARBARA. Cast, crew, technicians, everybody. Have them out here. In a semi-circle facing the set. Five minutes. I'm going. (*She leaves. Everyone starts talking and fooling around immediately, relieved that the tyrant has gone. Suddenly, Barbara reappears and shouts.*) Have them quiet! (*The cast freezes again, caught in the act. Barbara exits. The cast doesn't dare move for a beat, and then, when they are sure she is really gone this time, they go back to bedlam.*)

ELLEN. All right, folks. We need everybody out here. Everybody! Come on. (*To a cast member.*) John, go down to the green room, clear everybody out. (*Calling up to the tech booth.*) Come on down, you guys!

CHRIS. Ellen, how late are we going to be here tonight?

ELLEN. I have no idea.

CHRIS. We need sleep!

ELLEN. I don't know. Come on everybody, settle down, please. Barbara wants to talk to us.

JANET. (*Coming down from the tech. booth.*) She's going to line us up and shoot us all! (*The cast reacts with ad libs of agreement.*)

ELLEN. All right, folks. Quiet, please. Complaining won't help. Let's settle down.

MARLY. (*Entering with Stewart, from the back of the auditorium.*) Pardon me. Are you the director?

ELLEN. No, I'm the Stage Manager. This is a closed rehearsal. I'm not sure how you ...

MARLY. We need to see your director.

ELLEN. (*To the restless, noisy cast.*) Everybody, please have a seat. Be quiet. Help me out, here. (*To Marly.*) Okay. Barbara, the director, will be here in about two minutes. But I've got to warn you, she is not in the mood to talk to anybody but her cast and crew right now.

STEWART. Would you say your director is difficult?

ELLEN. What is this about? I would really like not to have to bother Barbara. (*To cast member.*) Careful of that costume, Annie! If you rip it, we're up the creek!

MARLY. We're from OSHA. (*At the mention of OSHA, everyone quiets.*)

ELLEN. OSHA?

STEWART. Yes. The Occupational Safety and Health Admini ...

ELLEN. I know what OSHA is. Listen, you guys came through six months ago. We fixed everything you asked. The rigging system will hold twenty elephants if needed ... safely!

MARLY. That's not our concern.

STEWART. We're actually from a new branch of OSHA. (*Handing Ellen a card.*) Theater Division.

ELLEN. (*Reading card.*) OSHAT? (*The cast laughs, repeating the word.*) You know, that sounds an awful lot like, "Oh, sh ... "

MARLY. We are well aware of the unfortunate acronym, and we are petitioning the home office for a change. That does not in any way diminish our responsibilities, however.

ELLEN. Just what are ... ?

BARBARA. (*From offstage, entering.*) Why do I hear talking? (*Everyone quiets. Barbara strides out, her eyes focused on the seated cast and crew.*) Miserable. Uncooperative. Lazy. Unfocused. I can't even get any relief when I go to the bathroom. Do you know why? Because I walk in and see the toilet and I am reminded of this production.

Now, I'm going to give you all three minutes. Three. In that time, you are going to make phone calls informing your loved ones — if you have any — that you won't be home tonight. (*The cast begins to groan.*) Oh, no — not a word! Not one word! You brought this on yourselves! Do you think you have any other possible person in this world you could blame ... (*Marly clears her throat loudly.*) Who are you and what do you want?

MARLY. Barbara Cramer?

BARBARA. Who wants to know?

MARLY. Marly Howe, Stewart Sparks. We're from the Occupational Health and Safety Administration, Theater Division.

ELLEN. OSHAT, boss.

BARBARA. OSHAT?

MARLY. And acting under the authority of OSHAT, we order this theater closed and all of its occupants dispersed.

BARBARA AND ELLEN. What?

STEWART. Go home, ladies and gentleman. You all look fatigued.

BARBARA. Wait a minute. Wait just a minute!

ELLEN. Everybody sit down, please. Let us get this cleared up.

MARLY. Are you defying an official OSHAT edict? Because if you are, you are in serious trouble.

BARBARA. You're damned right I'm defying your edict. I've got a show to put on here. Get the hell out!

STEWART. This is one of the worst violations I've ever seen. We've got to get these people out of here.

BARBARA. Over my dead body, you ...

ELLEN. Boss, hang on. (*To Marly and Stewart.*) Listen, could you please explain something before you call in a SWAT team?

NORM. OSHAT to SWAT. OSHAT to SWAT. (*The cast laughs.*)

BARBARA. That's not funny. That is not funny! There's nothing funny about tonight. Shut up!

STEWART. Marly, this is a class one emergency.

MARLY. It's all right, Stewart. Give me a second; we might be able to talk this one through.

ELLEN. Please. Marly, right?

MARLY. That's right.

STEWART. And I'm Stewart.

BARBARA. And I'm going to ...

ELLEN. Boss. Barbara. Let me figure this out. (*Back to the OSHAT people.*) Now, if you haven't come to look at the physical facility — which, I assure you, is as safe any theater in America — what is it you're ...

STEWART. Emotional safety.

ELLEN. Excuse me?

MARLY. OSHAT's prime directive is to insure emotional safety in the theatrical workplace. We were tipped off that your director, here, was using all manner of emotionally unsafe practices to, quote-unquote, motivate her charges.

BARBARA. I'll quote-unquote you, you beady-eyed platypus!

STEWART. Clearly, the tip-off was not inaccurate.

ELLEN. Wait a minute. Just a second, here, please. I think we can clear this up.

MARLY. I am completely confident we can. Eventually. In the meantime, I want this place evacuated.

BARBARA. You want evacuated? I'll give you evacuated, you overstuffed little shrew!

ELLEN. Barbara!

STEWART. (*To the cast.*) Ladies and gentlemen, if you will

please exit in an orderly fashion. You have OSHAT's personal guarantee that you will not be asked to return until the premises have been cleared of all emotionally-damaging elements.

BARBARA. You want to talk damage? I haven't even ...

ELLEN. Boss, please. You're making it worse.

STEWART. If you feel as if you need counseling to recover from your ordeal, there will be an OSHAT refugee center established within the next couple of days. Until then, I suggest you go home, take a soothing bath, have some tea or other hot beverage.

BARBARA. Did you hear that? We open tomorrow and he's offering hot beverages!

ELLEN. Barbara, do me a favor, will you, please? Go to your office and stay there for five minutes.

SANDY. Shouldn't we change first? I don't want to go outside dressed like this.

ELLEN. Five minutes, okay?

BARBARA. But ...

ELLEN. Go. Please. (*Barbara exits.*) Everyone, hold on. Hang on just a second. Don't leave.

MARLY. Miss, I think you have no idea how serious this is.

ELLEN. I have an idea, believe me.

STEWART. Think of it this way: it's as if the psychological floorboards of this stage are about to give up, sending all of these people crashing through to land in a bloody pile of torn flesh and jagged bones.

ROBERT. The floorboards are bad?

PETER. Let me out of here! (*A stampede begins.*)

ELLEN. No!

MARLY. Just an analogy, folks. A simile. Don't panic!

ELLEN . Stop, everybody! Please! Stop! (*She produces a blank gun, fires off two shots. Everyone but Marly hits the floor. Stewart lies down, covering his eyes with his hands.*) Now get back here and sit down! (*Everyone returns obediently.*)

STEWART. (*Recovering from the scare, crossing to Ellen.*) That is hardly a nurturing way to gather your cast.

ELLEN. Desperate times call for desperate measures. Listen, is there some way we could work this out? (*To cast.*) Everybody, take five, but don't leave the room. Relax where you are. (*They all collapse in a heap.*)

STEWART.   Marly, I'm not comfortable leaving these people here.

MARLY. Stewart, I think it's important that OSHAT not appear inflexible. I think we can hear what Ms. ...

ELLEN. Ellen. I'm Ellen.

MARLY. I think we'll be safe in simply hearing what Ellen has to say.

STEWART. In my opinion ...

MARLY. We're quite clear on your opinion.

STEWART. You interrupted me.

ELLEN. What if ... what if I promised that Barbara would no longer be an emotionally dangerous person? How about that?

MARLY. In my experience, such promises rarely prove viable.

STEWART. Especially when dealing with a personality as volatile as your director's. Her demeanor is like an unstable roof, creaking, ready any moment to collapse and crush or impale your cast members with broken rafters.

SALLY. The roof is caving in?

ELLEN. No! No ... relax, everyone. (*To Stewart.*) Would you mind cutting the dramatic comparisons, just for now?

MARLY. I'll go this far, Ellen. If your director can display emotionally safe behavior during the remainder of this rehearsal, we'll not close the theater. At this point.

ELLEN. Great!

MARLY. However, I have no illusion that you people are in a position to monitor your own adherence to this requirement. We will be staying to supervise the situation. (*Marly and Stewart move to sit in the front row of the auditorium.*)

ELLEN. Fair enough. Janet, go get Barbara, would you? Tell her we're back on again. Everybody, get ready for the opening of this scene; we still have lots to do. Let's go!

MARLY. Remember, Ellen ... at the first sign of danger, out you all go.

ELLEN. Out we go. Gotcha.

BARBARA. (*Entering.*) All right, Ellen, what's going on? Did you get rid of those two obnoxious vermin?

ELLEN. (*Out to OSHAT pair.*) "Obnoxious Vermin" is a pet name. Barbara uses it to refer to people that she holds in only the highest esteem. Isn't that true, Barbara?

BARBARA. What are you talking about?

ELLEN. (*Crossing to Barbara, whispering.*) You have got to make nice. OSHAT out there will not let this show go on unless you treat everybody very respectfully. No name-calling, no insults, no shouting.

BARBARA. I can do that.

ELLEN. You have to do that.

BARBARA. I can. (*Deep breath.*) Don't worry. (*Out to OSHAT.*) As Ellen was saying, "Obnoxious Vermin" has been a term of endearment used in our family for years. I can remember my dear old grandmother saying that to me as a child. Uh ... she would tuck me in and say, "Good-night, Obnoxious Vermin." Uh ... and then she would ... kiss me. She smelled like, uh, hay and toothpaste. (*Looking a bit nervously at Ellen.*) Right. (*To the cast.*) Okay ... good people. Let's go to Jason's entrance, final act of the play. Let's focus, now, you ... highly qualified professional types and we'll get a lot done. Here we go.

(*The scene begins with Claire on the floor, the wolves on top of her, the wind women swirling around, the drums and the noise at a very high pitch. Jason enters and shouts gallantly -- the wolves and the wind women run away.*)

JASON. Cybeline! Cybeline!
BARBARA. No! No, no, no!

(Barbara storms up on stage and runs to Jason. She is about to launch into a tirade when she sees Ellen signaling her to be careful. A major source of the humor of the play comes as Barbara employs various tactics of face and body twisting, twitches, stomping, heavy breathing, in order to keep from saying what she really wants to say.)

How ... ! How ... surprised I was, Jason, to see you come in yet again without a horse.

JASON. She told me it's still not ready yet.

BARBARA. *(After a long pause.)* That bothers me. I'm bothered quite a bit. Ellen. Oh, Ellen.

ELLEN. She's coming right up with the horse, Barbara. It's on the way.

BARBARA. Why in the he ... I'm disappointed that it wasn't here for Jason's entrance during this dress rehearsal the night before we open.

ELLEN. I ... *(Hetty enters, looking very distraught.)* Hetty! There you are.

HETTY. I'm sorry. I'm so sorry.

BARBARA. Sorry? Sorry is not a word I like to hear right now. I like to hear words like, "Barbara, the horse is all finished, and I think you're going to love it."

HETTY. I just ... I can't say that. It's no good. It's terrible. I've failed you; I've failed the show. The horse stinks!

BARBARA. Stinks? *(Getting the signal from Ellen.)* Uh ... well ... uh ...

STEWART. *(Coming onstage.)* Barbara, I commend you for your efforts thus far. Clearly, you are making attempts to change, crude as they may be.

BARBARA. Oh, thank-you.

STEWART. You are welcome. But let me help by adding to your communication toolbox, all right? Just like a carpenter can hardly do every job with just a sledgehammer, varied situations call for varied approaches, you see?

BARBARA. Sure.

STEWART. Now, you're Hetty, right?

HETTY. Yes. My horse should be shot.

STEWART. Now, Hetty, I understand that you're upset about a horse.

HETTY. Stupid horse. Bad, bad horse.

STEWART. *(To Barbara.)* Notice how we seek for understanding by paraphrasing the situation, you see?

BARBARA. Oh, yes.

STEWART. Hetty? Hetty, you are a worthwhile person. I know that. *(To Barbara.)* We validate the individual.

BARBARA. Validate.

HETTY. My horse looks like crap!

STEWART. But you, Hetty, are not your horse. Do you understand? You are not your horse. *(To Barbara.)* We separate the person from the product, lest she think an evaluation of her work is an evaluation of her self worth. Very important.

BARBARA. Oh, I can see that.

STEWART. *(Still to Barbara.)* Now, we seek to provide perspective. *(To Hetty.)* Hetty, Hetty, we are often our own worst critics. Rarely are things as bad as they seem.

HETTY. I detest my horse!

STEWART. But that need not keep us from loving it. Can we bring out the horse, please?

HETTY. No! *(She tries to run away, but Stewart tackles her.)*

STEWART. Hetty, stay here. It's all right. Barbara, call for the horse.

BARBARA. Get me the horse! Pretty please. *(The horse enters. It is truly horrible: two actors in a lumpy outfit that looks vaguely like a cross between a horse and a camel, both with some disfiguring illness.)*

JASON. I'm supposed to ride in on that?

HORSE BUTT. *(To Horse Head.)* You've got to walk with some rhythm. Do you know what rhythm is?

HORSE HEAD. Stop running into my butt!

HETTY. Look at it! It's terrible!

STEWART. I wouldn't say that. It's ... got a ... very ... a very ...

JASON. How do I even get on this thing? (*He tries to climb on the horse.*)

HORSE HEAD. Hey, get off of there. (*To Horse Butt.*) Ow! You pinched me!

HORSE BUTT. I did not! Why would I pinch you?

HORSE HEAD. I have no idea, but I'm warning you — cut it out!

JASON. Would somebody tell me what I'm going to do with this?

ELLEN. Jason, sit down for now. We'll figure it out.

HETTY. I failed!

STEWART. I have never seen a more ... thought-provoking horse. (*Hetty sobs.*)

HORSE BUTT. Move. Will you move? I can't stand like this; it's killing my back.

HORSE HEAD. Ouch! That's it ... that is the last straw, you. (*The two actors begin fighting inside the horse costume, turning into a writhing mass of random horse pieces.*)

STEWART. Barbara, as director, you are in charge of the morale of your cast and crew. Hetty clearly feels that her efforts are not pleasing. Go on. Say something encouraging to her. Compliment the horse. (*Barbara stares, open-mouthed, at what's left of the horse flailing on the floor.*)

HETTY. I know! Oh, Barbara, it's disgusting, terrible ... go ahead and yell at me. I know I deserve it.

HORSE HEAD. I'm never working inside an animal with you again.

HORSE BUTT. Who asked you to? You need rhythm for animal work. Rhy-thm. Ever heard of it?

HORSE HEAD. I'll show you rhythm, you ... (*They begin tussling again.*)

HETTY. I tried! I really did. But everything ... I'm so sorry, Barbara. It's the worst thing I've ever made!

STEWART. Barbara, Hetty is appealing to you for support.

Help her. Help her or forget the whole show, Barbara. (*The Horse tumbles off the stage. The two actors within groan.*)

BARBARA. (*Peering over the edge with Hetty.*) It's ... too good, Hetty. We couldn't possibly put such a ... work of art on stage. Somehow, we'll ... get along without the horse. Okay?

STEWART. (*To Hetty.*) There, you see?

HETTY. She's lying! She's lying just because you threatened her. She hates it! Any dolt could see that! (*Getting off stage and pulling the costume off the actors.*) Get out of here, you two!

STEWART. Hetty, we must learn to accept praise, to cherish it.

HETTY. (*Handing Stewart the butt portion of the costume.*) Cherish this. Barbara, I have let you down. I am turd on toast. I'll get out of your sight. Could you possibly scream at me, just once?

BARBARA. (*To Stewart.*) She's asking.

STEWART. Don't take the low road. Maybe what she really wants is a hug.

HETTY. All right, forget it! Just forget it. Again, I'm sorry. (*Grabbing the costume piece from Stewart.*) Give me that. (*She exits quickly.*)

STEWART. Barbara, don't be discouraged. I think you just made a great deal of progress. Carry on. Marly, this is going very well, I think. (*Barbara looks dazed.*)

ELLEN. Barbara?

BARBARA. (*Battling impending insanity.*) Okay. No horse. Jason, you just ... enter without the horse. Walk as if you've been on one, but you left it somewhere off stage. Yeah. Yeah. Okay?

JASON. I guess.

BARBARA. Good. Please. Thank-you. Now ... uh — let's begin the scene again. Okay? Okay, everybody? Bless you. Good. Please. Thank-you. Begin.

(*The scene begins as before. Jason enters, trying to follow*)

Barbara's direction about walking as if he's been on a horse.)

JASON. Cybeline! Cybeline! (*He crosses and kneels next to the "dead" body of Claire.*) Oh, my love; I fear I am too late. (*He takes her in his arms and begins to lift her, but she starts to giggle. Jason breaks character.*) What? (*Claire laughs openly.*) What is the problem? (*Claire starts laughing uncontrollably now, unable to stop.*) Barbara!

BARBARA. All right. All right. Okay. Please, thank-you, may I? Good. Let's begin again. And, Claire, I wonder if I might get you to ... not laugh. Okay?

CLAIRE. Okay. (*She almost breaks up again, but she keeps it in check.*) I'm all right. I'm fine. I won't laugh.

BARBARA. Let's ... can we ... just go from when Jason enters, how about that? Thank you. I beg your pardon. Thank-you.

TIMPANI PLAYER. From before his entrance? Do you want me to play?

BARBARA. No! I just said that we were taking it from ... ! You ... ! Let's ... take it ... from after, please, where you play? And all that. Okay? Begin.

(The scene begins again.)

JASON. Cybeline! Cybeline! (*But Claire cracks up again, just like before.*) What is so damed funny? Huh?

ELLEN. Claire, we do not have time for this. What is the problem?

CLAIRE. I ... I don't know! (*She starts laughing again, crying really, because she can't get it under control. Barbara growls, walks over, grabs Claire roughly, and looks her menacingly in the eye. Claire is quiet, as is everyone else.*)

STEWART. Barbara ...

ELLEN. Boss, remember.

BARBARA. When he goes to get you and pick you up in this scene, don't laugh. Thank-you. Please. (*Claire looks at Barbara for a long time, then cracks up again.)*

CLAIRE. I'm sorry! I can't help it. There's just something ... ! (*She's lost it again, falling on the floor. The other cast members start to get annoyed, telling her to shut up.*) I'm sorry. All right. I won't laugh. I'm done. Whew. There. I'm done.

BARBARA. You're sure?

CLAIRE. I'm sure. I can do the scene.

BARBARA. All right. Now let's just go from where Jason is bent over, picking her up. Can we do that? Claire?

CLAIRE. I can do that. No laughter. (*They go to that part of the scene. Jason picks her up. She cracks up. Everyone erupts in dismay.*)

CLAIRE. I can't help it!

STEWART. Barbara, it seems to me that Claire could use a very succinct "I statement" from you right now.

BARBARA. A what? Please, thank-you.

STEWART. An "I statement." Very helpful in sorting out conflict. Again, we're increasing the size of that communication toolbox. An "I statement" goes like this: "When you" ... and you name the particular behavior that is bothering you, then finish the sentence with "I feel ... " and here you name the specific reaction you have to that behavior. Try it. Say, "Claire, when you ... " Go ahead.

BARBARA. Claire, when you laugh during this scene ...

STEWART. That's right. Now move to the "I feel" segment.

BARBARA. I feel ... I feel ...

STEWART. Stay specific and constructive. Name your reaction.

BARBARA. I feel like I want to tear off your toes and feed them to a pack of rabid gerbils!

MARLY. That's it!

STEWART. That was not a productive comment!

BARBARA. You told me to be honest! That was honest!

ELLEN. Wait a minute! Wait a minute!

MARLY. This is an unsafe atmosphere! Everybody out.

Let's go! Up, up, up!

STEWART. You can't tell people you want to tear off their toes!

BARBARA. I'll tell you something, you ... (*Claire screams, so loud that everyone freezes.*)

CLAIRE. Thank-you. Since I was the cause of this latest disturbance, I would like to say something. May I? All right. I always laugh when I am nervous. It's a bad habit. I remember I used to do it even when I was potty training. My parents would stand over me, making me very nervous, waiting for me to do my thing, and I would end up laughing so hard that I fell off the toilet.

JASON. Your point is?

CLAIRE. My point, Jason, is that I am nervous now since we're supposed to open tomorrow. And there's something about the way you grab my ribs that sets me off. So I laugh. I can not help it; I've never been able to stop in the past — that is, until working with Barbara. Frankly, she has been so intimidating — up until you two (*Indicating Stewart and Marly.*) arrived — that I never dared laugh. But now, what with Barbara being such a warm fuzzy and the nervousness and all ... It's out of control again. That's what happened. I'm sorry. Everybody. I'm sorry.

STEWART. Claire, when you share so frankly with us, I feel like I want to be your friend.

CLAIRE. Thank-you, Stewart. When you tell me that, I feel like I might be sick.

STEWART. (*To Barbara.*) Do you see, Barbara, how freeing and productive this tool of communication can be?

MARLY. Stewart, I've seen enough. Let's move these people out of here.

STEWART. I've been so enjoying actually educating, Marly. I have felt empowered.

MARLY. Frankly, Stewart, I think you may be losing sight of our mission as OSHAT representatives. This is not about education nor about your personal sense of empowerment.

This is about safety. We need to get these people out.

BARBARA. Stewart, when you help me add to my communication toolbox, I feel as if ... I want to hire you on as a permanent staff member. Please. Thank-you. Marly, when you speak your mind about personal emotional safety, I feel as if I want to write a letter of recommendation to your supervisor. Thank-you. Please. Gesundheit. Claire, when you laugh, I feel frustrated, but since we do have an understudy for your role, I feel free to allow you your personal expressions.

STEWART. (*To Marly.*) We have made progress. This is definitely a kinder, gentler theater than it was.

MARLY. Maybe. All right. But Barbara, this is my last warning.

BARBARA. When you give me a last warning, I feel ...

MARLY. All right, I get the point. Everybody can stay. For now.

STEWART. Marly, could I have a moment with you?

BARBARA. Okay, then, Claire, Jason ... let's go back to where we left off. Positions, everyone. Thank-you.

MARLY. What's the matter?

STEWART. I wonder if you realize that you have interrupted twice this evening. Me once, and Barbara just a moment ago. Do you think this behavior sets a good example?

MARLY. I'm going to ask for a new partner.

STEWART. (*Following Marly back to the seats on the front row.*) Marly ... ?

(*The scene begins again. Jason gets Claire up into his arms this time, brings her downstage.*)

JASON. Oh, you Gods, why have you ... ? (*He stops because Claire is laughing again.*) Oh, for crying out loud! Barbara!

BARBARA. Understudy, please. Claire, why don't you take a nice long break, okay? How about that? Maybe a hot beverage, like Stewart suggested earlier.

ELLEN. Who's Claire's understudy? Where is she? Mary?

Mary, are you ready?

CLAIRE. I'll be all right. I swear.

BARBARA. Well, I know you will. But we need a non-laugher here. Okay? Thank-you. Bless you.

CLAIRE. I'm sorry. I'll stop. (*She lies down on the floor to prove that she can do the scene. Everyone watches. Claire squirms, biting her tongue, but she eventually ends up in another fit of laughter. Two cast members drag her away.*)

MARY. (*Wearing a wolf costume, pushed to Barbara by Ellen.*) I'm Claire's understudy. But I don't know the lines.

BARBARA. You don't ... ! Well, when you say that, I feel ... confident that you can learn them by tomorrow, okay? Pardon me.

MARY. I guess so. I don't know.

ELLEN. She'll know them, Barbara. She will.

MARY. I guess. I'm no good at memorizing.

BARBARA. Why don't you ... lie down so we can run this scene. You don't laugh, do you, when you're nervous?

MARY. I never laugh. I suck at memorizing lines, but I never laugh.

BARBARA. That's nice. Wonderful. Jason, shall we run the scene again?

JASON. First I don't have a horse, now I get laughed at.

BARBARA. Jason! The scene. Thank-you. So much. Good. From the top, okay?

TIMPANI PLAYER. You want me to play this time?

BARBARA. Oh, yes! Play! Do! Boom-boom! Play! Good! Now!

(*The scene begins, builds to where Jason reaches to pick up Mary. But she is too heavy, and they both fall in a heap.*)

JASON. Ouch! Ow ... she's too heavy! Mary, did you gain weight or something?

MARY. Screw you, Jason.

JASON. Barbara, I can't lift her. She weighs a ton!

MARY. You better shut up, Jason!

JASON. I'll throw my back out! First I can't ride a horse, and now you want me to pick one up!

(Mary jumps on Jason's back and starts pounding on him. The cast tries to break them up. Someone knocks over a large part of the set. Ellen exits. Stewart and Marly come up on stage. Barbara crosses to the timpani during the pandemonium, taking the sticks from the timpani player.)

MARLY. I told you we should have cleared these people out! Now look!

STEWART. I am not to blame! Barbara, Barbara, these people need you! Barbara! *(Barbara suddenly bangs loudly on the timpani, out of control. The chaos stops, all attention turned towards Barbara.)*

BARBARA. Mary had a little lamb, little lamb, little lamb. Mary had a little lamb, it's fleece was white as show. Show. *(She giggles.)* We open tomorrow. Barbara had a little show, little show, little show. Barbara had a little show and now it's gone to hell. *(Giggles again, then suddenly looks intently at a spot on the floor of the stage.)* Ooooo. Somebody dropped his lines. *(She starts to crawl around, looking for the lines. The cast members look at one another in dismay, ad libbing lines about Barbara's descent into lunacy.)*

MARLY. All right, everyone. We can delay this evacuation no longer. This building needs to be vacant within the next fifteen minutes, or we will be forced to take police action.

STEWART. It's been a pleasure working with you, but the time has definitely come.

JASON. Wait a minute. What about the show? We open tomorrow.

SHIRLEY. We're not ready! We need more rehearsal.

MARTHA. I'm not sure of my final entrance!

DONALD. What about the curtain call?

MARIA. We don't want to leave yet ... we've worked too

hard for this.

MARLY. This is for your own good!

BRIDGET. What about the good of the show?

MARLY. You have fifteen minutes. It would be a dereliction of duty to allow you to stay.

(From the back of the auditorium, a whistle. Ellen, dressed very heavily in military attire and makeup that masks her appearance, struts down the aisle of the auditorium, up onto stage.)

ELLEN. *(In a clipped German accent.)* Enough! I have seen enough. Cease and desist from your activities, if you please.

MARLY. Who are you?

ELLEN. I am Wilhelm Doppelganger Zeitgeist.

STEWART. What can we do for you, Mr. Zeitgeist?

ELLEN. *(Indicating Marly and Stewart.)* You and you can leave, that's what you can do for me. Immediately.

MARLY. I'm afraid you don't understand. We are from OSHA, theater division.

ELLEN. As am I.

STEWART. Excuse me?

ELLEN. Give me a hug. *(She hugs them both, sharply, without warmth.)* We are comrades; we work for the same organization, only I am more important.

MARLY. I don't ...

ELLEN. I am the reigning supervisor of the International Occupational Safety and Health Administration, Theater Division, a satellite society of the United Nations, Charter Member of North Atlantic Trade Organization, honorary delegate to The Oil and Petroleum Energy Cartel, major contributor to several political action committees, as well as to the United International Children's Education Fund and to the International House of Pancakes. My card.

MARLY. How can we be sure you're not an imposter?

ELLEN. Can you say the acronym?

STEWART. (*Reading slowly from the card.*) UNO ... uh, UNOSHAT ...

ELLEN. Perhaps you mean to say UNOSHATNATO-PACUNICEFOPECIHOP?

MARLY. (*To Stewart.*) He's legit.

STEWART. No question. I didn't even know we had an international division.

ELLEN. Now, I have been watching from the rear of the theater, having heard that you were planning a raid. I am appalled at your judgment.

MARLY. But ...

ELLEN. Ah! No interruptions. There is theater to be monitored in Siberia, if you understand my drift. Snow drift, that is. Ha, ha. Little joke at your expense. Listen carefully, while I tell you why you have no business being here. Now, you walk in for a few minutes and determine that this theater has emotional unsafeness in it, yes?

MARLY. Yes.

ELLEN. No!

STEWART. No?

ELLEN. No! You must look beyond appearances. (*During this sentence, the accent gets very thick — almost unintelligible.*) This organization functions on the very nature of the interplaying factors of passive interaggressionarianism and the overt display of introverted non-conformity to specified norms of tooth decay. Do you understand?

STEWART. Well ...

MARLY. Uh ...

ELLEN. You little American OSHATs. You never study. Have you not read and memorized UNOSHATNATO-PACUNICEFOPECIHOP's manual, Chapter 13, that covers just such a situation as this?

MARLY. I ...

ELLEN. Do not bother to answer. The faces on your expression tell everything. Simply, I suggest you leave. You have done enough damage. (*Referring to Barbara.*) Look at this woman, once a capable director, now for brain she has tapioca pudding. Barbara, listen to me. You are director, not malnutritioned dodo bird. Come back to us.

STEWART. I ... I don't know what to say.

ELLEN. Say nothing. Come here. One more hug before you go. I want you both to know that you are worthwhile human beings with much to offer the world. My only regret is that you are so stupid. Now go away. Be ashamed and go away. (*Stewart and Marly leave, exiting through the auditorium.*)

ELLEN. That's right. Go on. Do no re-enter. Do not look back. Shoo.

STEWART. (*Almost out.*) When he told us to go away, I felt hurt.

MARLY. Oh, shut up and keep walking.

STEWART. Marly ... ? (*They are gone.*)

ELLEN. Now, all of you. I am not done with you. Gather around. Quickly! (*The cast gathers apprehensively around Ellen.*) I have but one very crucial question for you. (*Ellen looks at them sternly, then removes a piece of her costume to reveal who she really is.*) How'd I do?

CAST. Ellen! (*They gather around to clap her on the back and congratulate her. Barbara, after being spoken to by "Zeitgeist," has been standing off to the side, looking dazed, reorienting herself after her trip to la-la land.*)

BARBARA. Ellen! (*Everyone freezes at the sound of Barbara's old commanding voice.*) Tell me something. You're clever enough to have taken over during all this. And you would have been nice enough to satisfy those two OSHAT toadies. So why didn't you just step in, move me aside?

ELLEN. Because, Barbara ... you're the boss. Welcome home. (*Barbara stands still for a moment, obviously moved. She looks around at the cast and crew, gives one final look at Ellen.*)

BARBARA. All right, you school of bloated guppies, we've got work to do! Hetty, you've got one more hour to come up with a horse — and I don't want one that looks like a camel with the mumps!

HETTY. But ...

BARBARA. Do it. We need a horse, not excuses.

HETTY. I'm on it, Barbara.

BARBARA. Claire, please laugh again. I dare you. Just try it. See what happens.

CLAIRE. I ... if you don't mind, I don't think I will.

BARBARA. Jason, you've been whining like a Chihuahua in heat. Knock it off.

JASON. Okay.

BARBARA. There's an ugly rumor floating around that we open tomorrow night, people. Somehow, we've got to turn what looks like a herd of stampeding aardvarks into something vaguely approximating a play! So ... positions, Act III, Scene 4! Go! (*With a wry smile, watching everyone scramble.*) Please. Thank-you. (*The lights go down.*)

* * *

OTHER TITLES AVAILABLE FROM BAKER'S PLAYS

KEEPSAKES

Pat Cook

Drama / 4m, 6f / Interior

Ever look at a family portrait and wonder what those people, posed and smiling, are really like? This family portrait shows you the inner workings of the Rogers family – how they deal with everyday things, how they deal with both happy and sad events which effect each and every one of them. These funny, poignant and all-too-human characters go through life the best way they know how.

Austin does his best to keep the house running smoothly, unless he has to take Pawpaw's trunk out of the basement. Mary Jo is outwardly pleased when son Mitchell gets engaged to Tish but explains "They're too young!" Her sister, Brenda, helps out by saying "Not any younger than you were when you got married." Brenda's husband, Dale, has his own advice for young Mitchell – "Marriage consists in large part of just giving up!" And Pawpaw keeps hearing voices and seeing people who aren't there.

The very fabric of the family unit meets its ultimate challenge when Brenda and Dale have to move in with them. Daughter Jan has to put up with a whiney dog, Mitchell and Tish can't seem to find time to talk about their upcoming marriage and everyone is bunking up with everyone else, leaving the men to sleep on the couch – any of this sound familiar? Brought to you by the same author of *Good Help is So Hard to Murder.*